I'm Going To READ!

These levels are meant only as guides;
you and your child can best choose a book that's right.

Level 1: Kindergarten–Grade 1 . . . Ages 4–6
- word bank to highlight new words
- consistent placement of text to promote readability
- easy words and phrases
- simple sentences build to make simple stories
- art and design help new readers decode text

Level 2: Grade 1 . . . Ages 6–7
- word bank to highlight new words
- rhyming texts introduced
- more difficult words, but vocabulary is still limited
- longer sentences and longer stories
- designed for easy readability

Level 3: Grade 2 . . . Ages 7–8
- richer vocabulary of up to 200 different words
- varied sentence structure
- high-interest stories with longer plots
- designed to promote independent reading

Level 4: Grades 3 and up . . . Ages 8 and up
- richer vocabulary of more than 300 different words
- short chapters, multiple stories, or poems
- more complex plots for the newly independent reader
- emphasis on reading for meaning

LEVEL 3

2 4 6 8 10 9 7 5 3

Published by Sterling Publishing Co., Inc.
387 Park Avenue South, New York, NY 10016
Text © 2006 by Harriet Ziefert Inc.
Illustrations © 2006 by Amanda Haley
Distributed in Canada by Sterling Publishing
c/o Canadian Manda Group, 165 Dufferin Street,
Toronto, Ontario, Canada M6K 3H6
Distributed in the United Kingdom by GMC Distribution Services,
Castle Place, 166 High Street, Lewes, East Sussex, England BN7 1XU
Distributed in Australia by Capricorn Link (Australia) Pty. Ltd.
P.O. Box 704, Windsor, NSW 2756, Australia

I'm Going To Read is a trademark of Sterling Publishing Co., Inc.

Library of Congress Cataloging-in-Publication Data

Ziefert, Harriet.
  Dancing class / Harriet Ziefert ; pictures by Amanda Haley.
    p. cm.—(I'm going to read)
  Summary: Polly Go Lightly practices her ballet positions and
dreams of dancing on the big stage.
  ISBN-13: 978-1-4027-3427-4
  ISBN-10: 1-4027-3427-1
  [1. Ballet dancing—Fiction. 2. Stories in rhyme.] I. Haley, Amanda, ill.
  II. Title. III. Series.

PZ8.3.Z47Dan 2006
[E]—dc22   2005034144

Printed in China

Sterling ISBN-13: 978-1-4027-3427-4
ISBN-10: 1-4027-3427-1

For information about custom editions, special sales, premium and
corporate purchases, please contact Sterling Special Sales
Department at 800-805-5489 or specialsales@sterlingpub.com.

I'm Going To READ!™

MORIOH

Dancing Class

Pictures by Amanda Haley

Sterling Publishing Co., Inc.
New York

Polly Go Lightly
hurries down the street,

carrying her dance bag—
she has friends to meet.

Polly Go Lightly
can unzip her zippers,

but asks the ballet teacher
to help her with her slippers.

Polly Go Lightly
has one hand on the barre.

She holds the correct position.
She wants to be a star.

"First position," says Madame.
"Now second with a toe.

Each position has its place.
Now point and off you go."

Polly Go Lightly
is learning what to do.

"Excellent," says her teacher.
"Now stretch and follow through."

"Everybody leap and spin.
Don't look at your feet!

Listen to the piano
to help you keep the beat."

Polly Go Lightly
leaps and twirls and spins.

Dancing . . . dancing . . .

. . . dancing!

See the smiles and grins.

Polly Go Lightly
sees Madame pirouette.

Then an arabesque and plié.
Polly hasn't learned them yet.

Polly Go Lightly says,
"I want to be the best.

And dance upon a great big stage
in front of all the rest."

Polly Go Lightly
has learned a lot today.

She curtsies to the teacher.
"See you next Saturday!"

first position

second position

third position

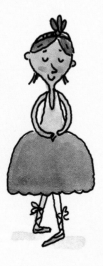

fourth position

fifth position

arabesque

plié

pirouette